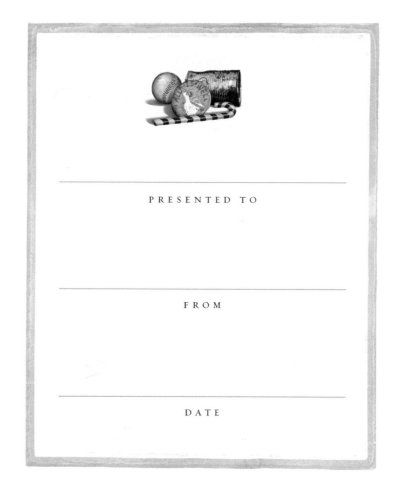

PRESENTED TO

FROM

DATE

TO: TIM *and* CINDY

ALL IS WELL

By Frank Peretti.

Illustrated by Gary Glover

Cover and interior design: The Office of Bill Chiaravalle, www.officeofbc.com

Published in association with Blanton, Harrell, Cooke & Corzine, Artist Management, Brentwood, Tennessee.

Library of Congress Cataloging-in-Publication Data

Peretti, Frank E.
    All is well / by Frank Peretti.
       p. cm.
    Summary: Hoping to earn money so that he and his mother will not have to move, Daniel goes around the neighorhood trying to sell a box of Christmas ornaments, including one with a special message.
    ISBN 1-59145-020-9
    [1. Single-parent-families--Fiction. 2. Neighborliness--Fiction. 3. Christian life--Fiction.] I. Title.
    PZ7.P4254 A1 2002
    [E]--dc21
                                                    2002027619

02 03 04 05 06 07 RRD 6 5 4 3 2 1

All *is* Well

THE MIRACLE *of* CHRISTMAS *in* JULY

Frank Peretti

ILLUSTRATIONS *by* GARY GLOVER

INTEGRITY®
PUBLISHERS
Nashville

It was July—there was no snow, no tinsel, no Christmas trees or carolers singing "Silent Night." It was summer, and the sun was hot. The folks in Daniel's neighborhood were busy with their lives. They were cranky from the heat. No one was thinking about Christmas.

6

uth, Daniel's mom, didn't want to think about Christmas either. Her husband, a kind man who loved her and Daniel, had died almost a year ago. So their last Christmas was not a happy time. Christmas had only reminded Ruth and Daniel of how lonely they were. So, Ruth had left thoughts of Christmas far behind—except for three little words she'd heard at Christmastime so long ago: All is well. She liked to say them often, whenever trouble came, whenever she felt sad. For some reason, those three little words brought her hope and lifted her spirits.

om, didn't you buy any Cheerios®?" Daniel asked when his mother returned from the grocery store.

"No," said Ruth, "but look at it this way: We saved money, and I didn't have to carry as much stuff home. I didn't have to carry Cheerios® or ice cream or popcorn or dish soap either. Just feel how light this grocery bag is!"

"Yeah, nice and light and easy to carry!" said Daniel, trying to see the good side of things.

"So all is well, right?"

"All is well," Daniel answered, barely above a whisper.

"That's the stuff! And besides, it won't be long before I get a raise at work, and we'll have a little more money around here."

"Then can you go back to nursing school?" asked Daniel.

His mom tried to look happy even though her eyes were sad.

"Well...no. I'll still have to work to pay the bills."

"I could work!"

"Thanks, but you're too little."

"I could sell stuff!"

"Honey, we've already sold everything that isn't nailed down."

ut Ruth was thinking about other things. "Did we get any mail?"

"I put it on the counter," said Daniel.

Ruth opened the envelope and frowned.

"What is it, Mom?"

"It's...well, it's a letter from Mr. Baynes, the man who owns this house."

"Oh-oh." Daniel had met Mr. Baynes once. He was grumpy and didn't like kids. "Is he mad?"

"Well, he wants money again, or we will have to move out."

Daniel thought of the old house they lived in. It creaked when they walked, leaked when it rained, and the old toilet was noisy. "Is that so bad?"

Ruth set the letter down and tried to look happy. "Oh, don't worry. We will make it somehow."

"So, can I?" Daniel pleaded.

"Can you what?" asked his mother.

"Sell stuff."

Ruth said, "Yes."

Very early the next morning, the neighbors could hear the rumble and squeak of Daniel's wagon. He was going from house to house, timidly knocking at every door.

Knock knock.

"Hi. I'm Daniel Preston from down the street. I'm selling stuff."

Abby Duvall, the plumber's wife, was still in her bathrobe, and the sunlight was making her squint.

"You're selling stuff? Looks like junk to me!"

"Yes, but it's good junk. Look at this."

"A coffee can?"

"You can keep things in it. Look, it's so shiny on the bottom you can see yourself."

Mrs. Duvall laughed, "I don't need any more empty cans around here."

aniel opened a large box full of mismatched, tangled, old and new sparkly surprises. "How about some Christmas ornaments?"

"In July?"

"You can use them later, can't you?"

Mrs. Duvall shook her sleepy head. "No, I don't want to think about Christmas. I have enough problems."

"Don't you want to buy anything?"

"Not today, kid."

And with that, she closed the door.

The rest of the morning didn't go much better. It seemed all the neighbors had plenty of junk already. And they had no time to talk to a little boy selling more of it.

"Dear God, you just gotta help me sell something. I don't want Mom to be sad," Daniel prayed.

onk honk!

It was Mr. Patrick in his old red truck. Daniel waved hello because friendly Mr. Patrick always waved back. This time he stopped and rolled down his window.

"Hi there, Daniel."

"Hi, Mr. Patrick."

Mr. Patrick had white, frizzy hair and a round, red nose. He would have made a good Santa Claus. He liked kids, too; he'd always let Daniel and his friends cross his yard to get to the woods. "What do you have in the wagon?"

"I'm selling special stuff today. Want to take a look?"

Mr. Patrick parked his truck and got out. He was dirty; he'd been working at the gardening store again.

"I've got a shiny coffee can or a nice egg carton. Or how about this can opener?"

"What's in the box?" asked Mr. Patrick.

"Oh, that's Christmas stuff. I guess it's the wrong time of year. Nobody wants to buy it now."

18

h, let me see it."

Daniel opened the box, and the sunlight danced across the silver and gold sparkles. Mr. Patrick carefully picked up each piece: a toy soldier, a teddy bear, a silver star, a paper chain.

Then he must have seen something that touched his heart. He picked it up and held it in his hand. Then he looked at Daniel with gentle, loving eyes. "Why are you selling all these things, Daniel?"

"So we don't have to move," said Daniel. "And Mom can go back to nursing school like she's always wanted."

"I'll give you ten dollars for the whole box," said Mr. Patrick.

Daniel couldn't even talk—his eyes and mouth were stuck wide open!

Mr. Patrick pulled out a crinkled ten-dollar bill and put it in Daniel's hand. "Merry Christmas."

"Ten dollars! Wait till I show Mom!"

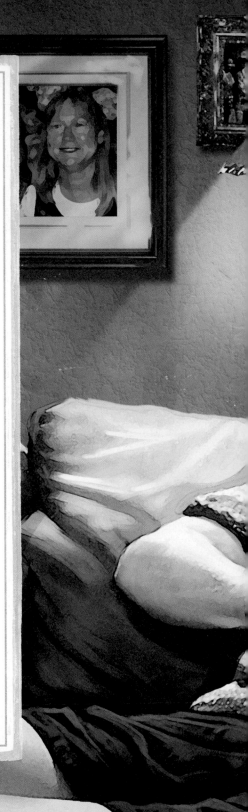

aniel threw open the old front door that wobbled. He ran across the old floor that creaked and found his Mom on the couch. "Mom! Look!" He held up the ten-dollar bill. "Now we don't have to move, and you can go back to nursing school!"

"Oh, Daniel! That's wonderful!" Ruth tried to sound cheerful. But her eyes were red, and Daniel knew she had been crying.

"What's the matter, Mom?"

"Oh, nothing. We are doing great, and you are really being helpful. Ten dollars! Wow!"

But Daniel could not feel good. He could only stare at his mother's sad face. "Mom, tell me how come."

"How come what?"

"How come all is well? You always used to tell me how come, every Christmas. Remember?"

"Well, of course, I remember. It's because..." But Ruth could not remember. She just sat there and could not say a word.

Knock knock knock!

When Mrs. Lloyd opened her front door, there was Mr. Patrick.

"Hello, Doris. And how are you today?"

Mrs. Lloyd was sitting in a wheelchair and was not feeling well at all. But she managed to smile at Mr. Patrick. "I'm OK, I guess."

"I suppose you have had a visit from little Daniel selling his special treasures?" asked Mr. Patrick.

"Sure did. But I am afraid I did not buy anything."

ell, Doris, I did buy something for you."

Mr. Patrick reached into his pocket and brought out a small, special treasure. He placed it in her hand. When she saw what it was, tears came to her eyes. She clutched it to her heart and smiled up at him. "You bought this from Daniel?"

"Oh yes."

"How could he possibly sell it?"

"So he and his mother won't have to move out of their house."

Mrs. Lloyd gasped.

Mr. Patrick nodded back. "I may need your help, Doris. May I call on you later? I have many other stops to make today."

Mrs. Lloyd looked once more at the treasure in her hand and replied, "Please do."

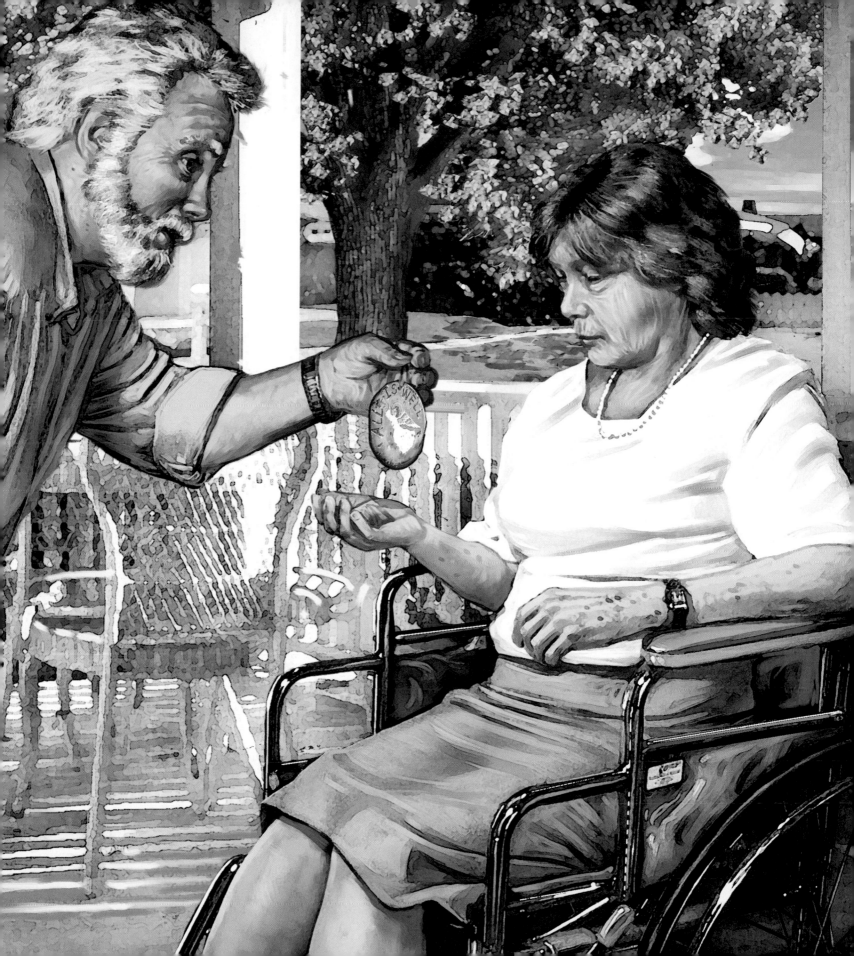

hat night, Daniel lay in bed unable to sleep. When his mother felt sad, he felt sad. And when ten dollars could not cheer her up, he felt even worse. When his eyes finally closed, he felt more than sad. He felt afraid.

The next morning, he sat in the empty kitchen eating the very last of the Cheerios®. He kept saying those same three words to himself: *All is well... all is well*. And he asked himself, *How come all is well?*

He thought of Mr. Patrick and the ten dollars. Then he remembered what Mr. Patrick said when he put the ten dollars in his hand: "Merry Christmas."

Daniel gasped. He dropped his spoon. His eyes grew wide.

When Ruth came in to say good morning, she saw the back door swinging. And she heard Daniel's footsteps running down the back steps. "Daniel! Daniel, where are you going?"

Too late. Daniel was gone, not looking back.

There was something Daniel had to find. It must have been in the box he sold. So off he went to Mr. Patrick's.

"Mr. Patrick, please, I need to buy back one of those Christmas things. It was a little dangly thing on a string, and it had glittery letters on it."

"The little clay one?"

"That's it!"

"Oh Daniel, I'm so sorry, but I don't have it anymore."

"You don't have it?"

"I gave it to Mrs. Lloyd. She hasn't been feeling well lately, and I thought it might make her happy. So I gave it to her."

Before Mr. Patrick could say anything more, little Daniel was running across to Mrs. Lloyd's house.

Knock knock knock!

"Mrs. Lloyd! Mrs. Lloyd!"

No one answered.

"Mrs. Lloyd, please!" Daniel started to cry. "Please, Mrs. Lloyd, I need to get it back!"

But Mrs. Lloyd was not at home. Daniel stood alone on her front porch with no one to hear his cries.

He finally returned home to their little, creaking, leaking house with the bare walls and peeling paint. His mother was waiting, sitting on the couch. She had no words, only open arms; so he climbed onto the couch and rested his head on her shoulder.

"Don't worry," she whispered. "All is well."

"I thought I remembered," Daniel said with tears in his eyes. "I wanted to show you how come all is well."

Oh dear God, she prayed silently, her arms around her son. *If you've given up on us, if you don't care about us anymore, then let me know right now because I can't go on acting as if you do care.* She sat there holding Daniel for a long time.

34

ap tap tap.

Daniel looked up, wiping his eyes.

"Hello?" came a voice. "Anybody home?"

It was Mr. Patrick!

Daniel jumped up. Ruth stood up. As they looked at the front door they could see Mr. Patrick's red nose poking in.

"Mr. Patrick," said Ruth, "come in."

The door swung open, and suddenly there was a loud and happy cheer, "MERRY CHRISTMAS!"

Ruth and Daniel could not believe what they saw. Mr. Patrick wasn't alone on their front porch. The Smiths were there, and so were the Dumbrowskis with the funny accents. And Mr. Ketcham, who carved wood, and Mr. and Mrs. Peringer from the big green house with the windmill were there too. And the Buxtons, who had that big white dog, and some other people Daniel didn't even know were there. But they were neighbors, every one of them. Daniel had seen their faces because he had knocked on all their doors.

e all got together and brought you a little some-thing," said Mr. Patrick, reaching back so Mr. Smith could hand him a shoebox. "We don't want you to have to move. We like having you here."

Ruth gasped, her hands over her mouth, and then she began to cry. Daniel was too small, so Mr. Patrick lowered the box so he could look inside. It was full of money—more money than Daniel had ever seen in his life. "Now we can pay Mr. Baynes!"

"That's right, Daniel," said Mr. Patrick. "Oh! And there is someone here to see you."

he crowd parted, and through the opening came an old lady in a wheelchair. Her eyes met Daniel's and her lips turned up into a smile. "Hello, Daniel. I'm sorry I was not home. I was at a very important meeting." Mrs. Lloyd looked around at her neighbors. "A meeting with all these wonderful people." She reached into her purse and brought out a small object. "I believe you were looking for this?"

Daniel took it from her wrinkly hand and showed it to his mother. "Mom! It's back!"

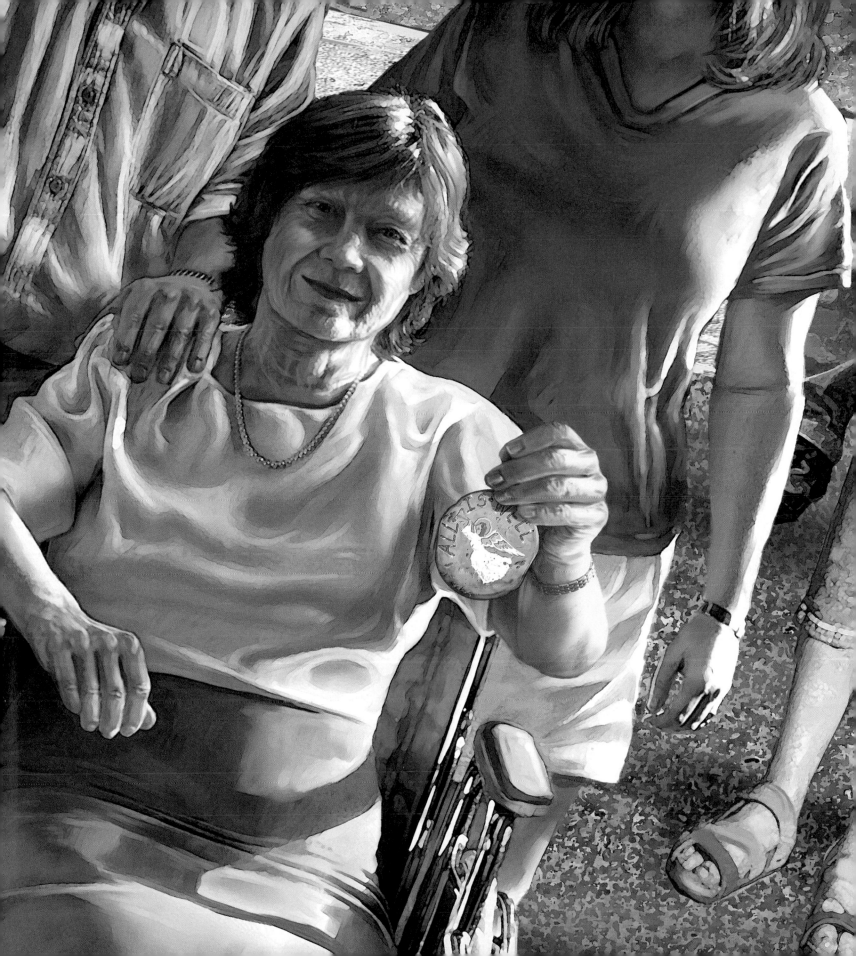

It was the little Christmas ornament—a funny shape of clay on a string. Ruth took it and gently turned it over in her hand. And some of her fondest memories came flooding back.

"Daniel, where did you find this?"

"It was in a box with some other Christmas stuff. I accidentally sold it to Mr. Patrick, and then he gave it to Mrs. Lloyd."

"And I am feeling so much better today!" said Mrs. Lloyd.

"We all are!" said Mr. Dumbrowski.

Daniel hugged his mother. "Now do you remember, Mom?"

Ruth remembered. Daniel's dad had made the ornament. Then Daniel had painted it when he was only three years old. It was shaped wrong, the paint colors were faded, but the message was clear.

On one side were those words, lovingly carved by Daniel's father: "All is well."

n the other side was the reason: "For unto us a child is born."

A sudden gleam of hope filled Ruth's face, and Daniel could see it. "All is well, huh, Mom?"

Ruth closed her hands around the little lump of clay and held on. "Yes, son, all is well."

Now that she remembered how come "All is well," Ruth knew she and Daniel would be all right. She could joyfully tell Daniel once again that our lives are like a story. And God is the Grand Storyteller, who knows the happy ending of the story from the very beginning. She could tell Daniel about a stable in Bethlehem so long ago. There God came to earth as a baby so he could be a part of our story. And he came to stay with us until our story is completed his way, in his name and for his glory.

And that's how come "All is well." Remember?